First U.S. edition 1992
First published in Great Britain in 1992 by Walker Books Ltd., London.
Library of Congress Catalog Card Number 91-58745
Library of Congress Cataloging-in-Publication Data
Sharratt, Nick.
Monday run day / by Nick Sharratt.—1st U.S. ed.
p.   cm.— (A Candlewick toddler book)
Summary: Simple rhyming text follows a dog through the days of the week.
ISBN 1-56402-092-4 (lib. bdg.) : $5.95 ($7.95 Can.)
[1. Stories in rhyme. 2. Dogs—Fiction. 3. Days—Fiction.]
1. Title. II. Series.
PZ8.3.S5323Mo   1992   91-58745
[E]—dc20
10 9 8 7 6 5 4 3 2 1

Printed and bound in Hong Kong

Candlewick Press
2067 Massachusetts Avenue
Cambridge, Massachusetts 02140

Monday Run-Day

by Nick Sharratt

CANDLEWICK PRESS
CAMBRIDGE, MASSACHUSETTS

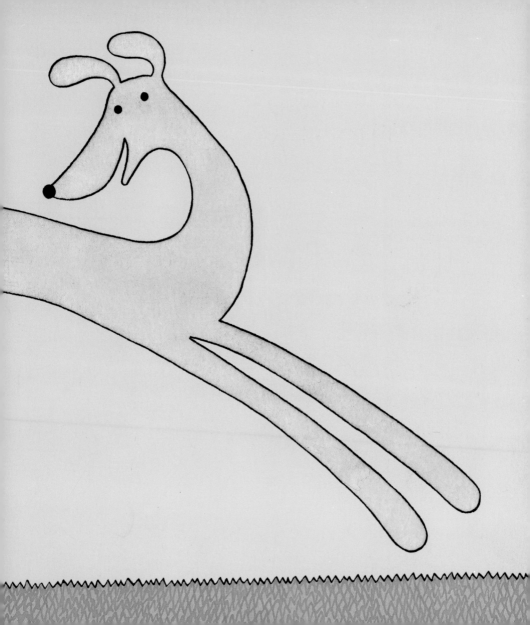

Tuesday
snooze-day

Wednesday
friends-day

Thursday
grrrs-day

Friday
tie-day

Sunday
bun-day